THE FLYING BEAVER BROTHERS AND THE HOT-AIR BABOONS

MAXWELL EATON III

ALFRED A. KNOPF
NEW YORK

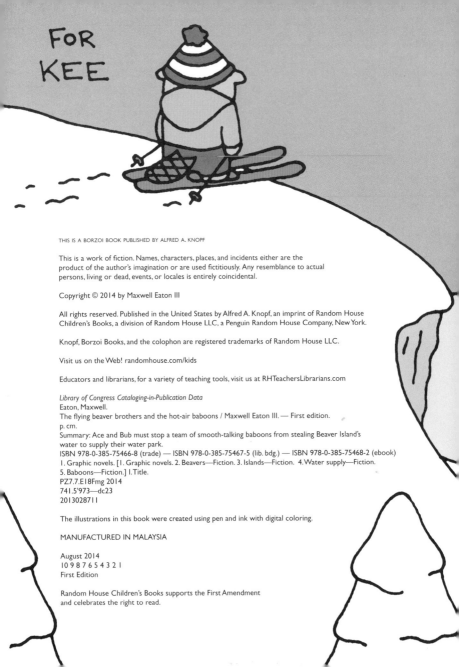

FOR
KEE

THIS IS A BORZOI BOOK PUBLISHED BY ALFRED A. KNOPF

Visit us on the Web! randomhouse.com/kids

Educators and librarians, for a variety of teaching tools, visit us at RHTeachersLibrarians.com

Library of Congress Cataloging-in-Publication Data
Eaton, Maxwell.
The flying beaver brothers and the hot-air baboons / Maxwell Eaton III. — First edition.
p. cm.
Summary: Ace and Bub must stop a team of smooth-talking baboons from stealing Beaver Island's water to supply their water park.
ISBN 978-0-385-75466-8 (trade) — ISBN 978-0-385-75467-5 (lib. bdg.) — ISBN 978-0-385-75468-2 (ebook)
1. Graphic novels. [1. Graphic novels. 2. Beavers—Fiction. 3. Islands—Fiction. 4. Water supply—Fiction. 5. Baboons—Fiction.] I. Title.
PZ7.7.E18Fmg 2014
741.5'973—dc23
2013028711

The illustrations in this book were created using pen and ink with digital coloring.

MANUFACTURED IN MALAYSIA

August 2014
10 9 8 7 6 5 4 3 2 1
First Edition

THIS DOESN'T SOUND RIGHT AT ALL. YOU GUYS WOULD BE RIDICULOUS TO BELIEVE ANY OF IT.

DO YOU HEAR THAT, EVERYONE?

HE'S CALLING US RIDICULOUS.

ME?!

CAPTAIN JOJO!

CAPTAIN JOJO?! THE MOLE THAT TRIED TO STEAL OUR ISLAND'S DIRT WITH A GIANT VACUUM BOAT?

ACE AND BUB? THE BEAVERS THAT SURF AND NAP AND LIVE ON BEAVER ISLAND?

WHY ARE YOU TALKING LIKE THAT?

I THOUGHT YOU WERE.

Swooooo